HANGIN' WITH JASON DOLLEY

AN UNAUTHORIZED BIOGRAPHY

BY GRACE NORWICH

PRICE STERN SLOAN
Published by the Penguin Group
Penguin Group (USA) Inc., 375 Hudson Street, New York, New York 10014, USA
Penguin Group (Canada), 90 Eglinton Avenue East, Suite 700, Toronto, Ontario
M4P 2Y3, Canada
(a division of Pearson Penguin Canada Inc.)
Penguin Books Ltd., 80 Strand, London WC2R 0RL, England
Penguin Group Ireland, 25 St. Stephen's Green, Dublin 2, Ireland
(a division of Penguin Books Ltd.)
Penguin Group (Australia), 250 Camberwell Road, Camberwell, Victoria 3124, Australia
(a division of Pearson Australia Group Pty. Ltd.)
Penguin Books India Pvt. Ltd., 11 Community Centre, Panchsheel Park,
New Delhi—110 017, India
Penguin Group (NZ), 67 Apollo Drive, Rosedale, North Shore 0632, New Zealand
(a division of Pearson New Zealand Ltd.)
Penguin Books (South Africa) (Pty.) Ltd., 24 Sturdee Avenue,
Rosebank, Johannesburg 2196, South Africa

Penguin Books Ltd., Registered Offices:
80 Strand, London WC2R 0RL, England

Photo credits: Cover: John M. Heller/Getty Images; Insert Photos: first page courtesy of Steve Granitz/
WireImage; second page courtesey of Frazer Harrison/Getty Images; John Shearer/WireImage;
third page courtesy of John M. Heller/Getty Images; Bobby Bank/WireImage; Albert L. Ortega/
Prphotos.com; fourth page courtesy of Dean Kirkland/Prphotos.com; Jeffrey Mayer/WireImage

Library of Congress Cataloging-in-Publication Data is available.

ISBN 978-0-8431-8927-8 10 9 8 7 6 5 4 3 2 1

HANGIN' WITH JASON DOLLEY

AN UNAUTHORIZED BIOGRAPHY

BY GRACE NORWICH

PSS!
PRICE STERN SLOAN

CONTENTS

INTRODUCTION

JASON CARES

As the sun rose over Los Angeles on April 13, 2008, it promised to be another scorcher in Hollywood. Some twenty miles northwest, Jason Dolley rolled out of bed in his home in Simi Valley and climbed into one of his favorite ensembles: distressed jeans and a short-sleeved baby-blue polo over a crisp, white T-shirt. For accessories he donned a cool leather cuff bracelet, silver rings, and a black string necklace. He checked his trademark California coif in the mirror, making sure the wispy, blond bangs were angled just so. It was a big day for Jason, and he wanted to make sure he was ready for it.

Back in the heart of Hollywood, at Universal Studios Hollywood, preparations were underway for a star-studded extravaganza. Inside the famous Globe Theatre, the tables were being decked out in silk tablecloths and elaborate, blown-glass centerpieces. A circus theme had been selected for the event, so everywhere you looked there were acrobats and stilt walkers practicing their routines up and down the corridors.

The party was elaborate enough to host Hollywood's most recognized red-carpet affair—the Academy Awards! But that celebration had actually taken place a few weeks earlier. No, the stars about to be honored were not Hollywood's biggest names. (Not yet, anyway!) They were, however, the industry's brightest up-and-comers, and in a few hours time they'd be receiving the awards to prove it.

There was Dominic Janes, star of the hit series *Out of Jimmy's Head*. And Madison Davenport, who'd recently wrapped up work on the movie *Kitt Kittredge: An American Girl*. Dominic and Madison and 150 others were not only ready to party, but also to receive their 2008 CARE awards, short for Child Actor Recognition Event. The award is really special because it goes to outstanding young actors who are mega-talented, have a 3.0 GPA or higher in school, *and* are active in community service.

Jason Dolley was one of CARE's cutest and most practiced honorees. As the confetti rained down around him at the party, Jason must have been feeling pretty good about himself. That's because this wasn't Jason's first CARE award, or even his third! This was the *fourth* consecutive time Jason Dolley had walked down the red carpet to receive the distinguished prize!

But if he was feeling like a prize himself, he didn't let on. Jason may be one of Hollywood's hottest young talents, but he doesn't let the attention go to his head. Instead, he took it in stride, just like he always does. "I love doing this—the red carpet and everything," he said to the *Los Angeles Daily News*. "It's a great experience.

It's easygoing and a lot of fun."

It's not surprising Jason has a whole rack of these CARE awards. He's awesome at pretty much everything he does. But you'd never guess it, because Jason is so humble that he never shows off. But check out these stats. At school, he maintains a perfect 4.0 GPA. That means straight As across the board! "I've always loved learning about the world around me and how things work and how everything works together," Jason told Scholastic News Online. Even though Jason is at the head of the class, he's not one of those annoying know-it-alls, always bragging about his grades. He doesn't brag about any of his accomplishments.

He also doesn't go on about how he's superinvolved in his community—even though he is. Some kids spend all their free time at the mall or hanging out with friends, but not Jason. When he's got a moment to spare, he's on the lookout for ways to help those less fortunate. That might mean spending an entire day at the local children's hospital with a project called Teen Impact where he and other kids have parties with family members. That would be enough fun to put anyone in a good mood. But for Jason, it's a serious commitment. "Groups of us will go room to room and every time I go, it hits me as a real wake up call," he told *PBS Kids*. "This is what these kids go through every day. They live in the hospital. Anything I can do for that is really cool. It really gives you perspective."

Another way Jason makes the world a better place is through his concern for the environment. His passion for environmentalism began when he first noticed the pollution in his California hometown. Ever since then, Jason has tried to find ways to clean up the environment. "Cutting off your shower time is really good. Even if you cut your shower time off by like a minute, it'll save so much water, and that's really cool."

Jason Dolley is definitely the full package: adorable, smart, talented, funny, and socially responsible. But with his usual modesty, he doesn't take credit for his accomplishments, but instead gives it to his parents. "I am very fortunate to have a loving, supportive family that has brought me up in normal circumstances," he told the *Detroit News.*

Jason does come from a pretty amazing family. But so do a lot of kids. And they don't all end up with a trophy case full of awards and starring roles in the hottest TV shows and Hollywood movies. There's something special about Jason.

CHAPTER 1

GROWING UP DOLLEY

On July 4, 1991, the city of Simi Valley in southern California had its usual Independence Day festivities. There were barbecues and parades up and down the pretty, tree-lined streets, all in celebration of the birth of the United States of America. But for the Dolley family, which at the time consisted of a mom and dad and three boys, the birth of the nation was the furthest thing from their minds. Instead, they were focused on the birth of their newest family member, who was scheduled to arrive at any moment. *Forget the fireworks*, the Dolleys must have been thinking: *We're ready for our little sister or brother to come into the world!*

One day later, on July 5, the Dolley family got their wish, in the form of an adorable baby boy, who would be christened Jason Scott. Life in the Dolley family—and eventually for all of Simi Valley—would never be the same. Because little Jason Scott was destined for very big things!

Jason was definitely the baby of the family, and he soon had everyone charmed by his adorable smile. But his older brothers never minded. There's always been plenty of love to go around in the tight-knit Dolley clan. Jason definitely brought a new energy to the family dynamic. The fact that his two eldest brothers, Ben and Larry, are around ten and twelve years older, respectively, may have something to do with Jason's comfort as an entertainer. Let's face it, when your siblings are that much older, you better be pretty darn entertaining if you want to get their attention.

His other brother Jeffrey is just one year older than Jason, so it's natural that they would have the closest bond. When Jason was a little kid, he and his brother often ended up as partners on the family stage. "Me and [Jeffrey] had these Batman and Robin pajamas and every now and then we'd put on a Batman show for our parents," Jason told the *Detroit Free Press.* "Looking back on this now, I don't even understand what we were doing . . . we didn't know what the plot was, we didn't know who our characters were, we were just in this movie."

If the Dolley parents had no idea what kind of show their two youngest sons were putting on, they didn't let on. As parents go, they're about as supportive as it gets. When a reporter from *PBS Kids* asked Jason who his personal role model is, he didn't hesitate. "Personally, honestly, I think my dad," he said. "Because he's done exactly what I want to do someday: He's created a great home environment, where if there's any tension, it's gone by the next day and everyone's really cool with everybody else."

The Dolleys totally supported their boys' theatrical sides, but Mom and Dad also exposed the kids to other activities—just in case the whole acting thing didn't work out! Simi Valley borders the San Fernando Valley, and is just a stone's throw from the beautiful Santa Susana Mountains. As a result, it's a nature lover's paradise, in close proximity to a ton of hiking trails and campgrounds.

It's no wonder that many of the Dolley family's favorite activities take place in the great outdoors. "All my life, my family has been camping freaks!" Jason said in *BOP* magazine. "Every year we go to the lake with a whole group of people." Jason has spent so much time in nature that he's full of advice about how to get the most out of the activity. "Definitely wear bug spray and try to go to the lake and do some fishing," he says. "If you're going fishing, wear a hat and some kind of sunglasses because the sun can get kind of annoying when you're sitting there!" Take it from Jason: he knows what he's talking about.

Simi Valley is beautiful and laid-back, which

explains why Jason is such an avid outdoorsman. But the community is also close to and very involved with Hollywood, which must have helped fuel Jason's love of acting. In fact, Simi Valley and its surrounding hills are frequently used as the setting for movies and television shows. For example, the hit 1982 film, *Poltergeist,* about a house that's haunted by evil spirits, was filmed on a street near where Jason grew up. Creepy! The same is true for the popular 1970s television show *Little House on the Prairie.* More recently, the skatepark used in the 2005 film *Bad News Bears* was located in Simi Valley. And much of the 2003 movie adaptation of Dr. Suess' *The Cat in the Hat* was filmed in Jason's hometown. That's a wide range of movies filmed practically right in Jason's backyard!

The list goes on and on. But suffice it to say that as a boy growing up in Simi Valley, Jason was definitely used to movie trailers rolling into town and movie stars delivering their lines in front of cameras and boom mikes. The buzz and excitement clearly had an impact on Jason. "I'd always wanted to be an actor since I was a little kid," Jason said to Kidzworld.com. "Whenever I watched a movie and I saw the main guy—you know, the cowboy riding in on the horse—I'd say to myself, 'I want to be that cowboy. I want to be the guy on the screen.'"

Jason and his brother Jeffrey continued putting on their amateur performances at home. They might have continued with the same Batman and Robin routine forever, but then, one afternoon, friends introduced them to another dynamic duo by the name of Abbott and Costello. Abbott and Costello were a couple of stand-up comedians from the 1930s and 1940s whose routines specialized in misunderstanding and confused wordplay. Seeing the famed comedy duo doing their thing on-screen had a real impact on Jason and Jeffrey. "Two of my friends introduced me to Abbott and Costello, showed me some of their movies, and me and my brother loved them," Jason told the *Fort Worth Star-Telegram.*

With their typical zeal, Jason and Jeffrey went home and watched every Abbott and Costello performance they could get their hands on. Eventually, they came across the comedians' most famous sketch, called "Who's on First?" In the routine, Abbott is trying to identify the players on a baseball team for Costello. The trouble is, the names of the players all sound like answers to Costello's questions. So the conversation gets more and more confusing—and comical. It's classic comedy at its best. Jason was hooked by "Who's on First?" from the first second he saw it, and that just happened to be right around the time of the school talent show. "We'd seen [Abbott and Costello in the movie] *The Naughty Nineties*, and that was one of the first times 'Who's On First?' was in a film," Jason remembered in the *Fort Worth Star-Telegram*. "So we saw that and we said, 'We gotta do that, we should do that for the talent show.' So we'd write down everything they said and practice it on the way to and from school. I was Costello—the dumb guy."

Jason must have been nervous the afternoon of the talent show. Not only were he and his brother tackling one of the toughest routines in all of comedy, they were doing it in front of the entire school! But to their relief, not to mention the delight of everyone in the audience, they totally nailed it! "Who's on First?" was Jason's first critical success. As he listened to the applause rain down from the audience, he knew that in the limelight was where he belonged.

He went home and declared his ambition to his parents: Jason wanted to become a professional actor. He'd always loved performing, but after that performance he knew he wanted to start pursuing a real career in acting as soon as possible. They were quick to embrace his passion and help him put his dreams into action. "The first thing we did was look for an agent," Jason told the *Detroit Free Press*. "It went remarkably smooth." It sure did! Just three months after signing on with an agency, Jason landed his first TV commercial, a national spot for the Kellogg's-brand cereal Smorz.

Jason followed up the cereal commercial by making an industrial video for the Discovery Channel. It wasn't anything that would be seen by wide audiences, but at this stage in his career, Jason was just trying to learn his craft. He understood from the beginning that acting is as much about hard work and determination as it is about looks and talent. Jason was born with plenty of charisma and star quality, but he still had to pay his dues. And filming anything, even an industrial video, helped build his resume and give him much-needed experience.

Some time after the Discovery Channel video, Jason was given the chance to read for a part in a short film called *Chasing Daylight*. This was not a bigwig from Hollywood knocking. Short films are usually made on a small budget and screened for limited audiences at film festivals. More than anything, they are a way for aspiring directors to prove their talents in the hope of getting a feature-length movie deal. But Jason recognized that if he got the job he, too, would be getting some great experience in front of the camera. Plus, he was going for the lead role in the film, the part of a young boy who is coping with the loss of his best friend. He decided to go in for the audition, even though it wasn't for a big-budget feature-length film. As with the Abbott and Costello routine, he hit a home run. The director offered him the part!

Even though *Chasing Daylight* wasn't a full-length feature film, shooting it was still very hard work. It called for long days on the set and doing take after take of every scene until they were all perfect. It was Jason's first taste of what making a movie is really like.

Fortunately, Jason had already proven himself able to handle discipline and hard work. At the school he was attending at the time in Simi Valley, Jason had already become one of the best students in the entire class. His favorite subjects at school, a private Christian academy, were science and Bible studies, but the truth is he excelled in all areas. So much so that he was chosen to represent the school in several academic competitions, including the spelling bee and the Math Olympics. "Oh, Math Olympics!" Jason recalled in Scholastic News Online. "It's a really cool experience, and they grade all the tests or whatever and they have an award show for who performed the best in each class, in each section. I think there were complications and word problems; there were two different kinds of—two denominations, I guess. Yeah, Math Olympics was fun!"

The concentration Jason learned in the classroom definitely served him well on the set of *Chasing Daylight.* It was a soul-searching part, especially for such a young actor. Sure, he'd been in several commercials and school productions, but being in front of the camera, with an entire film crew milling about, is a different process. Luckily, Jason never once buckled under the pressure. In fact, he only seemed to get stronger beneath it, which was a sure sign that he had chosen the perfect career path for himself.

Chasing Daylight was well received at numerous film festivals. Audiences enjoyed the story, and the director has since gone on to bigger and better projects. But the biggest buzz generated by the film was over the unknown child actor who played the lead part. No major awards went to the movie itself. But when the time came to decide the nominees for the Young Artist Awards for Best Performance in a Short Film, the blond sensation from Simi Valley by the name of Jason Dolley made the list. "I'm pretty proud of that one," Jason admitted to Kidzworld.com.

Jason's career was up and running. Just thirteen years old at that time, he was already winning praise from audiences and critics alike. But nothing could have prepared him for the big break that was about to come his way.

CHAPTER 2

A SAVAGE OPPORTUNITY

Every decade, the entertainment industry produces a new crop of talented actors who come out of nowhere to suddenly appear in every blockbuster film and on the cover of every glossy magazine. These are the actors who usually go on to have long, exciting Hollywood careers. Jason Dolley is definitely a break-out star of today. But back in the 1980s—before Jason was even born—the distinction belonged to a different group of big-screen celebrities. At the top of the list was a tough guy with handsome looks named Mel Gibson.

Gibson was one in a family of eleven children. He was born in the United States but grew up in Australia. He broke into the entertainment industry with his portrayal of a leather-clad renegade outlaw in the action classic *Mad Max*. Fans went absolutely nuts for tough but hot Mel. The film was such a hit that two sequels followed: *Mad Max 2* in 1981 and then *Mad Max Beyond Thunderdome* four years later.

The *Mad Max* series made Gibson a serious Hollywood contender. But his next role, playing the part of Sergeant Martin Riggs in the 1987 movie *Lethal Weapon*, made him an international superstar. By the time Jason was born in 1991, Mel Gibson was one of the biggest names on the planet.

When you reach megastar status, you can pretty much take on any project you want. Gibson is living proof of that. Throughout his career, he has been an actor, director, and producer on a diverse range of projects, including the controversial 2004 film *The Passion of the Christ*. The biblical movie, which was screened in movie theaters all over the world, was an incredibly intense project. It's not surprising that Gibson wanted to follow it up with something a little lighter. As luck would have it, two of his friends in the television business—the husband-and-wife writer/producer team of Julie Thacker-Scully and Mike Scully—were in the process of developing a television situational comedy, or "sitcom" as it's known in the business.

The Scullys are also no strangers to success. Among their credits were long-running hits like the family comedy *Everybody Loves Raymond* and the Fox animated series *The Simpsons*. But they were looking for something new. The couple has five children, so they thought it would be fun to create a series around a large family. That's when they remembered that Mel Gibson not only came from a huge family, but also had seven kids of his own! What followed was one of those lucky moments that almost feels like destiny in Hollywood. "We've been looking for a project to do [with Mel] for a while," Thacker-Scully told Zap2it.com at the time. "We both have large broods of children and we thought this was custom-made for us."

To make the show different from other family shows that came before it, and also provide plenty of comic relief, the Scullys decided to make the lead character a single dad named Nick Savage. Nick is a firefighter who is trying to make ends meet for his family, which might be an easy task if not for the fact that he's raising five unruly boys. The title of the show, playing off the last name of the main characters, would be *Complete Savages.*

Gibson loved the idea! He agreed to be the executive producer, but his involvement would wind up becoming much greater that just being the boss. "Mel actually had a lot of input on the show," Mike Scully told the *Deseret Morning News.* "He comes from a large family himself . . . The week we were shooting, he was in the writers' room every night pitching jokes." With Gibson on board, *Complete Savages* had a pretty good shot at becoming a hit series. With the scripts in place, they just needed actors.

Back in Simi Valley, Jason Dolley was plugging

away at school, going on auditions, and beginning to wonder if his big break would ever come. Fortunately, he had plenty of distractions at Grace Brethren Junior and Senior High School, the Christian school in town that he attended. First of all, there was his perfect 4.0 grade point average to maintain. Whatever free time was left over was spent playing paintball with friends, practicing hacky sack, or coming up with more tricks on another of his favorite pastimes, the yo-yo.

Jason definitely wasn't bored in Simi Valley. But at the same time, he was ready for a challenge. His agent must have been listening, because right around that time he came to Jason with news of *Complete Savages*, which was already being referred to as the "Gibson project" by industry insiders.

Jason was immediately intrigued by the part. And why wouldn't he be? After all, the premise of the show centered on a household full of rowdy, mischievous boys. They might as well have been talking about the Dolley household! What's more, the part Jason would be trying out for was the youngest brother, named T.J.

If Jason had written the script himself it couldn't be closer to his actual life. He knew that he had to have that art, so he told his agent to sign him up for the next audition!

Jason's agent managed to get him the audition. Jason took over from there, dazzling the producers. Of course, the producers loved him and quickly offered him the role. Jason accepted, and would be joined by an equally talented group of costars. The part of the dad went to Keith Carradine, a veteran actor of film, TV, and stage who has show business in his blood. With a famous Hollywood legend, John Carradine, as their dad, Keith and his two brothers David and Robert all became professional actors. Carradine was joined on *Complete Savages* by Shaun Sipos, an actor who had appeared on *Smallville.* Sipos played the cool older brother. The family jock would be played by Erik von Detten. Andrew Eiden played the middle son. And Evan Ellingson landed the part of the biggest troublemaker of the bunch.

There was plenty of excitement on set as everyone

gathered to film the first episode. Jason had been waiting for this moment his entire life. Sure, he'd nailed every commercial and amateur film he'd been in, but this was network television! ABC had optioned the show, so with any luck his face was going to be appearing on prime-time television within a matter of weeks.

As if the pressure wasn't enough, Jason and the rest of the crew were given the news shortly before taping began that none other than Mel Gibson would be directing the first episode! The biggest moment of Jason's young career got a whole lot bigger with the announcement. If he was feeling the nerves before, now he could hardly speak. Impressing Mel Gibson could definitely open some doors. But blowing it in front of Mel? That could be the end of his career. He really wanted to make a good impression.

Jason wasn't the only one really feeling the pressure. "I had just seen *The Passion of the Christ* right before I went into the auditions, so I didn't know what to expect," costar Andrew Eiden told Zap2it.com.

"The final audition, it was, like, me doing my thing in front of 40 people. And then there's Mel right in the center of them . . ."

Fortunately, Gibson is nothing like the crazy, intense characters he often plays in movies. In fact, according to Jason, he's just the opposite. "I imagined him as, like, a serious guy . . . totally into himself and all that," Jason told Zap2it.com. "But when I met him, he wasn't like that at all. He was . . . light, funny, he was really hilarious. He's really a big kid." Andrew agreed: "He starts cracking jokes and being really cool and it just totally lightens the mood," he told the *Deseret Morning News*. "He was just a really good guy. I think he's a wonderful actor and director, because I think he understands the point of view of the actor really well because he's such a good actor, too."

Once the ice was broken on set, Jason and the rest of the crew had a blast taping the first season of *Complete Savages.* The fun they were having definitely translated on-screen, as the Savage brothers get into all sorts of trouble, like the Thanksgiving episode where they try to help out by cooking a live turkey! Let's just say it doesn't go well. Jason's character, T.J., is often at the center of the hilarity, especially since he's totally obsessed with farts! All of that physical comedy was really fun on set.

Complete Savages premiered on ABC on September 24, 2004. Jason was just thirteen years old and already starring on network television. It was a big accomplishment. And even though he was one the youngest members of the cast, he definitely held his own. In fact, Jason was so good that when awards season came around, he was nominated for a Young Artist Award for Best Performance in a TV Series. Jason's costar Evan Ellington was also nominated. But when it came time to hand out the award, Jason was named the winner!

The sitcom itself also racked up a few award nominations, namely for a prestigious People's Choice Award for Favorite New Television Comedy. Each week, more than six million viewers tuned in to watch Jason and the rest of the stars on *Complete Savages.*

That's a pretty decent-sized audience, and by the end of its first season there were some signs that the show was gaining in popularity—which made it all the more shocking when the network decided to cancel the show.

Jason was devastated. After years of hard work, he was finally making it as a professional actor. Now, out of nowhere, the executives at ABC had splashed a bucket of cold water on his dreams. But as heart-breaking as the cancellation of *Complete Savages* was for Jason, it taught him about the fickleness of show business. One week you might be the hottest actor on television, and the next you're back on the audition line. The truth is, six million viewers might seem huge to most people, but a successful network TV show usually wants to bring in at least double that number. *Complete Savages* just hadn't caught on the way ABC had hoped.

Complete Savages may have ended in disappointment for Jason, but he didn't regret the experience for one second. In fact, according to Teenmag.com, Jason's most prized possession is a script signed by Mel Gibson and the entire cast. The final episode of *Complete Savages* aired in June 2005. When actors are out of work, they're sometimes said to be "resting." That's the industry term for it. Jason might have thought he was going to spend the summer of 2005 in resting mode. But even though *Complete Savages* hadn't been picked up by the network for another season, Jason's reputation had already spread well beyond the ABC studios. He should have known he wouldn't be out of work for too long!

As luck would have it, producers from another studio were working on a pilot for a new television show. A pilot is the term for a test episode of a potential television series. Of the dozens of pilots that get made each year, only a handful make it into prime time. But for a budding star like Jason, pilots are a great way to get more experience and meet other players in the industry. So when his agent called him up with an audition opportunity for a pilot called *Enemies*, Jason was all for it.

Enemies is the story of two best friends who grow

up in the same neighborhood but end up leading very different lives as adults. One becomes an officer of the law, while the other becomes a ruthless mobster. Jason read for the part of the mobster as a young boy. This was new territory for Jason, who until then had really only played nice characters. The directors must have been wondering if he had enough emotional depth to pull off the part. Of course, Jason blew them away with his performance. The part was his! Unfortunately, *Enemies* never made it to the small screen. Still, the experience was incredibly valuable for Jason's development into a true actor. "Up until the pilot for *Enemies*, I'd play the nice boy," he told Kidzworld.com. "But in *Enemies*, I was Mickey Holloway, a bad guy who grows up to be a mobster. That was a very different role for me and it was really fun—so I think I might be looking for the bad guy roles because they're a lot of fun to play." That might sound like a weird idea of fun, but a lot of actors like to play bad guys because it challenges them.

After the experience of *Complete Savages*, Jason

knew not to despair over the fact that *Enemies* wasn't picked up. He was really maturing as an actor. And sure enough, he wouldn't have to wait long for his next opportunity.

In Jason's next project, he played the sweeter-than-pie character Conner Kennedy in the Disney Channel original made-for-television movie *Read It and Weep*. Based on the novel by Julia DeVillers, *Read It and Weep* is the story of a girl named Jamie Bartlett who keeps a journal filled with juicy observations about all the kids at her school. One day she accidentally turns the journal in as a homework assignment. At first, she is rewarded for her talents as a writer. But when it emerges that all her musings are based on real people, she is forced to make amends with everyone she offended, including her best friend, Conner.

Jason only had a supporting role in *Read It and Weep*, but making the movie was a huge step in his career. First of all, it was his first time working with the Disney Channel, which has been responsible for making the careers of so many superstars, including

Miley Cyrus, the Jonas Brothers, Zac Efron, and Ashley Tisdale. Jason had always wanted to work with Disney, so he jumped at it when they offered him the role. Working on *Read It and Weep* was also pretty cool because of the movie's amazing cast. Jason got to star opposite the fantastic Panabaker sisters, Kay and Danielle, who played the parts of Jamie and her alter ego Is. The Panabaker girls were already seasoned Disney stars. Kay was one of the stars of the popular television series *Phil of the Future* and appeared in the made-for-television movie *Life is Ruff.* Danielle starred in the made-for-television movie *Stuck in the Suburbs* and on the big screen in Disney films *Yours, Mine and Ours* and *Sky High.* Both girls are also beautiful, talented, and supersmart. Jason was definitely lucky to have them as costars for his first made-for-television movie and he loved working with them.

Jason no doubt spent a lot of the downtime between shots asking the Panabaker girls about their experiences in show business. Chances are that Danielle and Kay didn't mind the attention. After all,

Jason was turning out to be one of the cutest boys in the business. Little did they know that his star was only starting to rise!

CHAPTER 3

HOLLYWOOD COMES CALLING

As far as acting jobs go, a career in television definitely has its advantages. First and foremost, the work is steady, especially for actors who are lucky enough to land a role on a popular, long-running series. TV stars also have the potential to reach a wide audience, given the fact that they come on every week in the living rooms of many homes across America.

Starring in television is a great way to start out as an actor. But deep down inside, most small-screen actors secretly long for their chance to make it on the

big screen. Why wouldn't they? Let's face it, while the life of a TV actor is hardly a struggle, the glitz, the glam, and the red carpet treatment is often reserved for movie stars. So, for the most part, are the multi-million-dollar contracts!

In 2005, the fourteen-year-old Jason Dolley wasn't worried about pulling in seven-figure movie deals. As long as he had enough cash in his pockets to purchase a new hacky sack or a new item for his skater-cool wardrobe, he was happy. But even without any strong desire for money, Jason was starting to set his sights on a career in movies. It might have had something to do with the time he had spent with Mel Gibson on the set of *Complete Savages.* Being in the company of a star of that caliber tends to rub off on a young actor. It's not so much the high salaries they rake in as the enormous influence they command. When Mel Gibson walks into a room, *everyone* notices. When he makes a suggestion, more often than not it ends up getting done that way. That definitely left an impression on Jason.

Beyond the power and prestige that comes with

being a major movie star, there's also the artistic satisfaction. Today's television is better than ever, thanks in part to cable television, which is responsible for many of the shows that sweep up the awards at the annual Emmy Awards. But the smartest, most creative minds in show business still gravitate toward the movie biz. The big budgets afford filmmakers much more creative freedom. This fact, more than any other, is what appealed to Jason. He knew that to reach his full potential as an actor, he'd have to find success on the big screen.

Fortunately, Jason's agent agreed, and was on constant lookout for just the right movie role. This can be a challenge for a young, up-and-coming actor. On the one hand, they need to appear eager and able to take on any role. But on the other hand, they don't want to appear in some awful, low-budget movie and risk jeopardizing their reputation as a serious performer.

Jason had already proven himself to be an extremely gifted actor, with not one, but two Young

Artist nominations to prove it, and even though he had only been in show business for a few years, the casting agents in Hollywood definitely knew his name. So it was only a matter of time before he'd catch his big break.

For Jason, the long wait must have felt like an eternity. But then one day, the phone finally rang. It was his agent calling with a great opportunity. The producers at Warner Bros., one of the biggest studios in Hollywood, had decided to make a movie called *Saving Shiloh.* And guess what? They wanted Jason to read for the leading role!

Saving Shiloh is actually the third installment in a trilogy written by a famous American author named Phyllis Reynolds Naylor. The stories center around a sweet-natured, intelligent boy named Marty Preston with a big heart and his dog, an adorable beagle named Shiloh. The series is set in a quiet town in the country, where Marty lives with his parents and kid sister. In the first installment of the trilogy, Marty rescues Shiloh when he is just a pup from an abusive neighbor named Judd Travers.

The third and final installment of the *Shiloh* trilogy delves more deeply into Judd's character. We learn that he was the victim of an abusive father, and that deep down inside he means well. Marty—a caring, soulful young man—befriends Judd and fights for his salvation. This becomes particularly difficult when Judd is named as the prime suspect in a local murder case. Everybody in town assumes Judd is guilty. So it's up to Marty to clear his name.

Jason must have felt an instant connection with the character of Marty Preston. Like Marty, he is an intelligent, thoughtful boy who grew up in a supportive home. And like Marty, he loves to be surrounded by nature, going back to the camping trips and hiking expeditions he took with his family from an early age. Last but not least, Jason understands the bond that exists between a boy and a dog. Jason has always been an animal lover. He once even had a pet rat named Sky! You have to really love animals to love a rat. But the love of Jason's life from the animal kingdom is a chocolate Labrador named Jasmine. Whenever he gets home to Simi Valley, Jason and his dog are practically inseparable. Whether they're playing catch in the backyard or going for long walks in the surrounding countryside, Jason and Jasmine are BFFs.

Considering how much Jason had in common with the character of Marty, it's no wonder that he nailed the audition. But it still must have been totally exciting when the producers called to say he had landed the part. After a seemingly endless wait, Jason was going to star in his first feature film!

The movie was shot on-location in the beautiful backwoods of Missouri. Jason had not spent much time in the Midwest before the film, nor had he been away from home for such an extended stretch. Fortunately, he was accompanied by his mother, Michelle, who joins him on just about every project. Jason and his mom are very close so he loves having her on set with him. In fact, when *Seventeen* asked Jason which family member he is closest with, he answered right away, "My mom. I can tell her anything and she won't react until I'm done

telling her *everything.* She'll kind of just sit there and observe, which is one of the many things she has to offer." Awwww.

In addition to his mom, Jason also had a second family in the form of his fellow cast members. Making a movie is a lot like being at camp. Actors are thrown together, often in a remote location, for weeks on end and forced to live together—just like a family. Sometimes they get along and sometimes they fight like cats and dogs! Fortunately, Jason was blessed with a cool and understanding crew on his first feature film. The cast included Taylor Momsen, who played the part of Marty's best friend, Samantha Wallace. Besides being a supersweet girl, Taylor is also an extremely talented actress. She got her big break playing Cindy Lou Who in *The Grinch Who Stole Christmas*, and has since gone on to star in the hit television series *Gossip Girl*, where she plays the role of Jenny Humphrey.

Jason had an awesome time filming *Saving Shiloh.* After the final scene was shot, he went home to California really believing that he had helped make a great movie. Of course, actors often think that. Then the movie comes out and it's panned by critics and ignored by audiences. So the weeks before the May 2006 release of *Saving Shiloh* were anxious ones for Jason. What if his first movie was a box office bomb? What if the critics gave him terrible reviews?

As it turned out, Jason had no reason to worry. Roger Ebert, one of the most famous (not to mention toughest) movie critics in the country gave him a glowing syndicated review: "Everyone involved in the film obviously had respect for the family audiences they are aiming at, and it's surprising how moving the film is, and how wise, while still just seeming to be about a boy and his dog, his family and the mean man next door who isn't so mean, if you get to know him."

Reading Ebert's review must have made Jason feel pretty good, but that was just the beginning. The *New York Times* critic Anita Gates wrote that "*Saving Shiloh* is touching, intelligent and admirably thoughtful," while Sheri Linden, writing for the *Hollywood Reporter*, made special mention of the "sympathetic performance by Jason Dolley" in her review of the film. The *New York Times* and the *Hollywood Reporter*—those are serious big-time publications!

Those kinds of reviews normally go to actors with years of experience in Hollywood. The fact that Jason got them on his very first movie was an amazing accomplishment. He could definitely be proud. But as people say in Hollywood, you're only as good as your last picture. So before *Saving Shiloh* had even left the theaters, Jason was already angling for his next project.

Once Jason had his first taste of moviemaking, he really wanted to focus on film. He wasn't totally against television, but he was more eager to develop his film career. "I think I prefer film," he told Kidzworld.com. "In film, you do a movie and you meet a bunch of people, and throw yourself into a character. When it's over, you get to meet new people and play new roles and have completely new experiences."

Jason's next project would definitely afford him a

wide array of unique experiences. He landed a small part in a very unusual movie called *The Air I Breathe.* The premise of the film is based on an ancient Chinese proverb in which life is broken down into four basic emotions—happiness, sorrow, pleasure, and love. The four main characters in the movie are based on these emotions. The film received a lot of hype for its unusual plotlines and large ensemble cast. It was a really big deal for Jason to win a role in a movie like *The Air I Breathe*, and he was very excited!

Whereas *Saving Shiloh* was a very straightforward narrative, *The Air I Breathe* takes all sorts of twists and turns. To be exposed to this kind of original storytelling at such an early stage in his career was very valuable for Jason. It made him realize that there's more than one way to tell a story. And that as an actor, the more versatile you are, the more opportunities you'll have throughout your career. Plus, *The Air I Breathe* introduced Jason to some seriously big-name actors. "The cast is HUGE," he told Kidzworld.com. "Big, big names, such as Brendan Fraser, Sarah Michelle Geller, Kevin

Bacon. Unfortunately, I never really got to work with any of them, but I did get to meet Brendan Fraser, because I play the younger version of him." The cast also included several Oscar-worthy performers, including Forest Whitaker (who took home the Best Actor award for his performance in *The Last King of Scotland*) and Andy Garcia, whose performance in *The Godfather III* earned him a nomination for Best Supporting Actor.

The Air I Breathe also meant Jason's first time making a movie in a foreign country—Mexico, to be precise. "That was a great experience," he explained to Kidzworld.com.

A great experience indeed! Over the course of two short years, Jason's film career was flying high. He was earning rave reviews from critics, starring opposite some of the best actors in show business, and traveling all over the world to hone his skills in front of the camera. Hollywood was hungry for more from its newest acting phenom. Jason was definitely excited to develop his reputation on the big screen. But he hadn't abandoned his roots in the small screen. Which was a good thing, considering he was about to land a plum part on one of the hottest shows on television.

CHAPTER 4

JASON IN THE HOUSE!

Most of Jason's younger fans really recognize him from his role on the hit Disney series *Cory in the House.* The show first aired on January 12, 2007, but that chapter in Jason Dolley's life actually began four years earlier, in January 2003. Jason was still getting his acting career off the ground at that time. He'd done a few commercials and was gearing up for his first short film. But his major successes were still a few years away.

Since Jason's schedule wasn't yet jam-packed with auditions and film shoots, there's a good chance

that he caught the January 17, 2003 premiere of a new Disney show called *That's So Raven.* New series on television are pretty common, since the network executives are constantly looking for the next smash hit. And the execs are quick to pull the plug on a show they don't think is connecting with audiences. In fact, a new show will sometimes be canceled after just a few episodes while posters advertising its arrival are still plastered all over billboards and bus stops.

Jason was becoming wise to the ways of show business, so he knew not to get too excited about any new shows. But there was something special about *That's So Raven*, and Jason wasn't the only one who noticed. From its very first episode, the show struck a chord with audiences and critics alike. The star of the series, Raven-Symoné, definitely had a lot to do with its appeal. The Atlanta-born actress, who is six years older than Jason, is one of the biggest talents of her generation. She practically oozes charisma. In fact, the series was originally going to be called *Absolutely Psychic*, but once Raven was tapped for the lead part, the producers decided to name it after her. Smart idea.

Besides its supertalented star, *That's So Raven* had a compelling plot. Raven-Symoné's character, named Raven Baxter, has psychic superpowers that allow her to see into the future. Raven doesn't always like what she sees, so she tries to alter the future, often with disastrous (and hilarious!) results. Raven's two best friends, Eddie Thomas and Chelsea Daniels (played by Orlando Brown and Anneliese van der Pol, respectively) and her younger brother Cory (played by Kyle Massey) are usually involved in the hilarity.

Audiences were smitten with *That's So Raven* from the very beginning. Within a few seasons, it had become one of the highest-rated shows in Disney history, with millions of fans tuning in each week to watch. The critics were equally impressed, and *That's So Raven* received numerous awards nominations, including the Emmys, Nickelodeon Kids' Choice Awards, NAACP Image Awards, and Teen Choice Awards.

Despite the enormous success of *That's So Raven*,

nothing lasts forever in show business. And so, on November 10, 2007, the final episode aired. Fans of the show were devastated. So were the Disney executives, who were losing one of their most popular shows of all time.

When a wildly successful show comes to an end, television executives often look to create a spin-off. That's the term for a new series that's based on one of the supporting characters in the original. Disney had never attempted it before, but *That's So Raven* had brought in so many viewers that they decided to give it a shot. But which character would they base the spin-off on?

After much debate, they decided that Raven's younger brother Cory, played by the talented Kyle Massey, had the best potential to carry his own show. *That's So Raven* fans adored Cory, with his mischievous ways and love of money. In order to give the show a fresh look, Disney decided to move the Baxter family from San Francisco to Washington, D.C., where Cory's dad, Victor Baxter, lands a job as the head chef at the

White House. That's a pretty cool move! The title of the show, playing off the Baxter's new place of residence, would be *Cory in the House.*

Back in Simi Valley, California, Jason was getting used to his new life as a movie star. The success of *Saving Shiloh* was still fresh in his mind, and he was still giddy from the experience of playing a young Brendan Fraser in *The Air I Breathe.* Still, part of him missed the camaraderie of television. Even though *Complete Savages* had only run for a year, he really liked seeing the same cast members week in and week out.

As a result, when Jason first heard about the new Disney project called *Cory in the House*, he was intrigued. Like a lot of other teenagers in America, he'd been a huge fan of *That's So Raven.* While Raven-Symoné was not going to be a regular character on the spin-off, Jason had heard she would probably return for guest appearances. That really got his attention! Not only is Raven-Symoné beautiful, she's also a major star. Jason had to be a part of the show!

As you know by now, when Jason goes after something, he usually gets it—whether it's straight As in school or the acting job of a lifetime. *Cory in the House* would be no different. From the moment Jason walked on set, the show's producers knew they had their Newt Livingston, the cute young son of the United States chief justice. Newt is kind and super-cool, although he's not exactly the brightest, which is ironic considering in real life Jason is at the top of his class. That was fine with Jason, who likes the challenge of playing different characters. "The first thing people will ask is, 'Are you really dumb, like you are on the show?'" Jason told the *Fort Worth Star-Telegram*. "I'm like, 'No, no, that's just Newt.' It's fun [to play a character different from yourself] because you get to make up stuff about the character." Plus, Newt is pretty cool! "My character Newt is like a rocker guy," Jason explained in *Popstar!* "He's supposed to go to school in a helicopter." Now that's high flyin'!

Newt is also a little bit of a loner. "Newt is an

heir to a political dynasty," Jason explained to Scholastic News Online. "His parents have always been in politics, but he's totally not into politics. Going into the family business is the last thing on his mind. He is a rocker. He plays the guitar. He's a very musical person. The truth is that he's sort of in his own world." Jason may not be exactly like Newt in every way, but he went on to say that, "I think he would totally be a friend of mine . . . We dress similarly. He's a guy who would be a lot of fun to hang out with." Jason's so nice, he could be friends with practically anybody.

Cory and Newt are joined in the White House by several other kid characters. There's Meena Paroom, the daughter of the Bahavian Ambassador. Maiara Walsh, a beautiful American actress of Brazilian descent, plays the part of Meena. Then there's the president's daughter, Sophie Martinez, played by Madison Pettis. Lastly there's Jason Stickler, son of the CIA's top spy and constant tormenter of Cory, Newt, and Meena. Stickler is played by Jake Thomas, who fans of the Disney hit show *Lizzie McGuire* will recognize as Lizzie's younger brother, Matt.

The cast of *Cory in the House* even included some performers from the animal kingdom. In fact, Jason's very favorite episode called for a star who normally hangs out underwater! As he told TeenHollywood.com, "I think 'The Presidential Seal' was absolutely my favorite because the seal was so much fun to work with. We didn't get to interact with him too much. It's got to be freaky for a seal to work on a soundstage in the first place. They brought him in in a big old truck and we had to clear out so there was a clear path for the seal to get into the set." How's that for a guest appearance?

That's So Raven succeeded in part because the cast had such amazing chemistry. From the first taping of *Cory in the House*, it was obvious that the same positive feelings would continue with the spin-off. "On the set, a lot of the crew had been together from working on *That's So Raven* and some of us were new members, but by the second season everyone was all a big family," Jason told *PBS Kids*. "For sure, everyone was friends with everyone. It's very intense during the week, we all spend so much time together, then on the weekends we go home and see our other friends. It's a good balance."

Taping a television show is exhausting work, and *Cory in the House* is definitely no exception. According to Jason, practical jokes are a good way to relax. "Most of the pranks are between Jake Thomas and Maiara Walsh," he confided to *Newsday*. "Throughout one episode they were kind of having a prank war going on. It was pretty low-key until Jake poured hot sauce on her food when she wasn't looking." But it was Maiara who apparently got the last laugh. "The next night it was his birthday, and the cake was brought out in front of a live audience. Maiara got a piece of cake and smashed it in his face." And what about Jason's involvement? "I'm usually on the sidelines watching the pranks," he admits. "I don't usually get involved because I'm not very good at them."

Jason may not be an expert prankster, but there is plenty that he is good at on the set of *Cory in the House*—including helping the writers and directors make every episode the best it can be. "They are very open to ideas," Jason told TeenHollywood.com, although with his usual modesty he gave more credit to his costar. "I think Kyle is probably the one who comes up with the most on rehearsal days. He's the one that's ad-libbing all the time. Usually, what he comes up with is funny and is in the next draft of the script." Jason isn't one to brag, but he's made plenty of contributions as well.

Jason definitely has a lot of respect for Kyle, who in a sense is the heart and soul of *Cory in the House*. "Kyle is a very cool person," Jason told Scholastic News Online. "He's always on. He's got energy all the time and I don't know where he gets it all. And he brings that to the show and to his character. He's very professional and he's a really cool person to work with."

Since joining the cast of *Cory in the House*, Jason has been inspired by Kyle and his other talented costars to pick up several new skills. For one episode, he even had to learn the Riverdance, a traditional Irish form of dance. "There's an episode . . . where Newt is part of a secret Riverdancing club in school," Jason told the *Fort Worth Star-Telegram.* "It's hard. It's like a cardio workout all day. I rehearsed for like three or four hours one day, and I went through like three or four shirts. Each one was drenched with sweat." That's commitment!

In another episode, Newt shows off his guitar skills for his friends in the White House. If Jason thought learning the Riverdance was difficult, it was nothing compared to playing the six-string. "I wish I could actually play what Newt plays on the guitar," Jason explained to TeenHollywood.com. "Most of the stuff in the middle of the second season, I was able to figure it out but I kind of wish it was actually me playing the guitar. I started playing when we started doing the show because I thought it was a good idea to have a basic feel of the guitar and look like I knew what I was doing." Since that episode, Jason has hardly put the guitar down. "I'm playing it all the time," he told *BOP.* "It's in my hands every chance I get. I'm always playing around between takes on the show and learning new stuff."

Between the new friends Jason was making and the many new skills he had to pick up, he was busier than he'd ever been in his life. In fact, he had so much to do that keeping up with his studies in school was proving difficult. For a straight-A student, this was hard for Jason to accept. So he made the difficult decision to leave the private school he'd attended for most of his life and get homeschooled instead. This is actually fairly common among young television stars, since their schedules are so hectic.

Jason still misses seeing his friends from school every day, but he loves his new education. As he told *PBS Kids*, "Being homeschooled is awesome because you can make your own schedule, so as far as time management, it's up to you how much you get done and when you get it done. It's all got to get done; how you do it is up to you. You need a lot of self-discipline, but luckily I have it." If Jason hadn't already been a straight-A student, who knows if his parents would have let him leave his traditional school. But he had already proven himself as an exemplary student.

Joining *Cory in the House* was a major adjustment for Jason, but he made it smoothly. And although part of him missed making movies, the show's first season was a tremendous success. Jason had taken a chance by returning to television, but it was paying off in a huge way. He was being watched in millions of homes each week. Everywhere he went people recognized his face and knew his name.

The awards were still rolling in as well. For the 2008 season, *Cory in the House* was nominated for an Image Award in the Outstanding Children's Program category. And Jason was nominated for his third Young Artist Award for Best Performance in a TV Series. Most importantly, the big shots at Disney knew that they had discovered a special talent in Jason Dolley. With stars like Zac Efron and Corbin Bleu getting older, they needed someone new to carry on the Disney tradition. Jason was only too happy to oblige.

HANGIN' WITH JASON DOLLEY

JASON ON THE RED CARPET FOR THE PREMIERE OF DISNEY'S *RATATOUILLE.*

JASON AND FELLOW *CORY IN THE HOUSE* STAR MADISON PETTIS ARRIVE AT THE WORLD PREMIERE OF DISNEY-PIXAR'S *WALL-E.*

JASON SIGNS AUTOGRAPHS AT THE 2007 POWER OF YOUTH EVENT TO BENEFIT ST. JUDE CHILDREN'S RESEARCH HOSPITAL.

JASON AT A HARLEM GLOBETROTTERS BASKETBALL GAME IN L.A.

WHAT A HOTTIE!

JASON CHILLS WITH FELLOW DISNEY STAR JAKE T. AUSTIN AT DISNEY'S *HIGH SCHOOL MUSICAL: THE ICE TOUR.*

JASON WITH THE CAST OF ABC'S *COMPLETE SAVAGES.*

JASON SHOWS OFF HIS *GUITAR HERO* SKILLS AT THE 2007 POWER OF YOUTH EVENT TO BENEFIT ST. JUDE CHILDREN'S RESEARCH HOSPITAL.

CHAPTER 5

DOLLEY GOES TO DISNEY

The Walt Disney Company is one of the most powerful media and entertainment companies on earth. What started in 1923 as a simple animation studio has evolved into a multibillion-dollar corporation. Today's Disney does it all, from movies to music to video games to television shows.

How did Disney get so big? The company has made a lot of smart decisions in its eighty-five year existence. But the biggest factor by far is its knack for spotting and developing talent. If you look back at all the young stars who have broken onto the scene in recent years, most of them have come up through Disney. Miley Cyrus, Britney Spears, Justin Timberlake, Lindsay Lohan, Ashley Tisdale, Zac Efron, and Vanessa Hudgens all got their start on Disney.

Cory in the House was Jason Dolley's first real introduction to the magic of Disney. For the first time, he saw up close how the company operates like a big family (one of the most talented and fun families in the world, that is!). Just about every cast member had worked on at least one other Disney project, so they were all up on the latest gossip and they all knew what exciting new shows and movies were on the horizon.

Jason was welcomed into the Disney club with open arms. But he had yet to land a lead role in a Disney project. Sure, fans loved his portrayal of Newt on *Cory in the House*. But until he was the star of a production, he wouldn't be a true Disney player. Fortunately, the executives at Disney were well aware of Jason's talents. In fact, they were just waiting for the right project to come along for him.

In 2007, a made-for-television movie called *Minutemen* got the green light (aka the go-ahead) from Disney's content developers. Described as an action-sci-fi-comedy, *Minutemen* is the story of three high school seniors who figure out a way to travel back in time. At first, their plan is to use the time-traveling machine to buy a winning lottery ticket, but after more discussion, they decide instead to go back in time to prevent embarrassing things from happening to their classmates.

The leader of the trio, who refer to themselves as the Minutemen in order to keep their time travels secret, is a likable teen named Virgil Fox. As a freshman, Virgil had experienced his own embarrassing moment when some upperclassmen left him hanging from a statue wearing a cheerleader's outfit. Four years later, Virgil is still trying to live down the experience, rather unsuccessfully. The time machine, he realizes, offers a way to make the humiliation like it never happened in the first place. Of course, nothing is ever as simple as it seems, especially where time travel is involved.

When Jason first read the *Minutemen* script, he knew he had to have the part of Virgil. It would be his first lead role in a Disney production. Plus, Jason actually saw a lot of himself in Virgil, so he knew he could play the part better than anyone. "The thing about playing a character closer to yourself, like Virgil is to me, is that you don't have to make that up, so it's easier to do," Jason said in *Fort Worth Star-Telegram.*

One of the biggest things Jason and Virgil have in common is supreme skill in math. "It's not extremely difficult for me," Jason told Scholastic News Online, somewhat modestly (remember his 4.0 average!). Jason may be good at math, but Virgil is "absolutely a math whiz," Jason explained to Scholastic News Online. "He comes up with the idea of quantum acceleration, I believe it's called. And he uses that on his rocket cart when he's driving around on the football field the first day when they are trying out for football. But then he also uses the quantum acceleration when he creates the time vortex, which is what allows us to go back in time. I don't know what quantum acceleration is, but it must be pretty powerful. I wish it existed." Jason is good at math—but not *that* good.

Jason had plenty to relate to in Virgil. Just as expected, Jason rocked the audition. The part of Virgil Fox was his! Unfortunately, the shooting schedule overlapped with *Cory in the House*, so he would have to leave the show for a few episodes. But the producers and rest of the cast were all very understanding since Jason was leaving them for another Disney project.

Jason must have been sad to leave Kyle, Maiara, and the rest of the gang from *Cory in the House*. But he was about to meet a whole new array of Disney talent, starting with the producers who would be making the movie. Disney had had so much success with their previous made-for-television movies *High School Musical* and its sequel *High School Musical 2* that they decided to bring in the same Emmy-winning producer, Don Schain, for *Minutemen*.

In true Disney fashion, Schain and his production

team drew from past Disney successes in their approach to *Minutemen*. For a location, they decided to use Murray High School in Salt Lake City, Utah, the same school used in the *High School Musical* films. As it turned out, Murray High was also used for some of the scenes in *Read It and Weep*, which Jason had shot a few years earlier. So he was on a familiar set. That's always helpful for an actor.

It's not surprising that Schain decided to shoot *Minutemen* in Salt Lake City. So far, nineteen Disney films have been shot in the state of Utah, further proof that when something is working for Disney, they really stick with it. The arrangement works for Utah as well, which charges Disney to film there. In fact, Disney paid Murray High School $18,000 to shoot there for seven days, and then donated another $5,000 when the filming was complete! That money could buy a lot of books!

The *Minutemen* producers also went back to a familiar group of actors for Jason's supporting cast. For the part of Charlie Tuttle, the boy-genius who figures out how to create the time-traveling machine, they tapped a talented young actor named Luke Benward. Prior to *Minutemen*, Luke was best known for his performances in *How to Eat Fried Worms* and *Because of Winn-Dixie*. To play Zeke Thompson, the gearhead responsible for building the time machine, Disney picked another of its emerging talents, a good-looking actor named Nicholas Braun. Braun was already a Disney name. He starred in the 2005 film *Sky High* opposite Danielle Panabaker, whom Jason knew from the shooting of *Read It and Weep*.

The love interest in *Minutemen* is a character named Stephanie Jameson, who was best friends with Virgil before she became part of the popular crowd. Disney chose an actress named Chelsea Staub for the part. Staub was best known for her work in theater, starring in such classical stage productions as *Peter Pan*, *Cinderella*, and *The Sound of Music*. But she had no trouble relating to the modern storyline of *Minutemen*, perhaps because she had so many of her own embarrassing moments to draw from. "One time in PE class in the sixth grade, we were playing softball," she told *McClatchy* newspapers. "I actually hit the ball, which I thought was great. As I began to run to first base, a pair of my underwear fell out of my pants leg. It must have been in my pants after my mother washed my clothes." That *is* embarrassing!

Last but not least, the cast of *Minutemen* included an actor named Steven R. McQueen, grandson of the great Hollywood legend Steve McQueen. He was chosen for the role of Derek, the school jock and boyfriend to Stephanie. Prior to *Minutemen*, McQueen played the part of Kyle Hunter in the hit television series *Everwood*. But he's best known for his relationship to his grandfather, who starred in the classic films *The Magnificent Seven* and *The Great Escape* and was known by the nickname The King of Cool. That's a pretty hard act to follow. "People mention it all the time," Steven told the *Washington Post*. "I guess being compared to him could be a burden, but I use it to help me give my all."

All in all, Disney had pulled together an awesome

cast for the production of *Minutemen*. Jason was feeling pretty confident when he reached Salt Lake City that the shoot would be a blast. And he was right! "*Minutemen* was a cool experience because everybody on the cast bonded and were friends really quickly," he told TeenHollywood.com. "The first couple of days we were going to dinner together. Off-camera, Dexter Darden who plays Chester, one of the nerds, was a riddle genius. I love riddles. I was solving them and coming back for more. Everybody on the set got into it, too." Jason got along well with all of his castmates, although some of them gave him a hard time about his special acting techniques! Jason has been known to rub his cheeks right before shooting a scene. It helps Jason get into character, but everyone on set thought it was hilarious!

The set of *Minutemen* was a lot of fun, but the cast had to work hard, too. Filming took place in the middle of summer, so the days were long and hot. That was especially true for Jason, Luke, and Nicholas, since the script called for them to be in snowsuits whenever they traveled through time. Fortunately, the snowsuits were fitted with cooling vests, but it still got hot in them. Jason also had to put on a pair of fake braces, since Virgil wears them. "I got fake braces fitted before we started shooting," Jason explained to TeenHollywood.com. "I actually still have them. They won't fit anybody else so they thought they might as well give them to me. I can use them in a Halloween costume somewhere down the line. [In real life] I have removable braces. They look like retainers. I take them out when I work. It's a hassle."

Between the snowsuits and fake braces, not to mention the many stunts called for in the script, Jason was working harder than ever. But as the days unfolded, Jason and his cast members became more and more confident that they were making a truly great movie. Not only was the cast great, the story was one that people would connect with. "This is a movie that you can keep in the DVD player," Jason later told the *Detroit News*. "People can relate to the characters. It has a real feel to it."

The Disney executives were feeling confident as well that *Minutemen* would connect with a wide audience. "[*Minutemen*] deals primarily with issues that are real in kids' lives," Michael Healy, senior vice president of Disney said in the *Washington Post*. "We look at the question of identity. 'What is it like to grow up? Can I still be myself and have friends?'"

The *Minutemen* script definitely tackled real issues facing teens today. But it was also packed with plenty of humor. Fortunately, Jason had really worked hard at honing his comedic talents on *Cory in the House*, so his timing and delivery were right on the money in every scene. The directors must have been impressed by this relatively young actor's nose for comedy. Little did they know he'd been developing his skills for years, all the way back to the renditions of "Who's On First" that Jason used to perform with his brother for crowds of a few dozen classmates back at his school in Simi Valley.

It's a good thing Jason had such a developed sense of humor, since the script required his character to be in some pretty embarrassing situations. The worst of all was when Virgil and Charlie get hung out to dry (literally!) in one of the opening scenes. "I think that the most difficult scene to film but probably that's going to be the funniest on-screen was the scene where Luke and I are hanging from the lamb statue," Jason admitted to Scholastic News Online. "I've seen pictures and it's just hysterical, it's really unlike anything I've ever seen before... So it was kind of difficult to be up there and just kind of, like, knowing that everybody is staring at you and you're in this cheerleader outfit but you try not to think about it."

Other actors might have crumbled under the embarrassment of that scene, but not Jason. He's such a secure person in real life that he can roll with the punches anytime he's in front of the camera. It's a good skill to have. "You have to take that with a grain of salt because that's part of the deal with comedy; making a complete fool of yourself," he told TeenHollywood.com. "I kind of started getting used to that on *Cory in the House*. But that's probably the most embarrassing kind of stunt. It was pretty wild hanging up there. But, nobody was making fun of me in the cheerleader suit. You try and focus on the scene. And then once you're down, you kind of just try to forget about it. Yeah, I think that was one of the most difficult scenes to film."

Minutemen also has plenty of excitement and suspense. What audience can resist a good old-fashioned time-travel flick? At one time or another, everyone fantasizes about what they'd do or redo first if they discovered a portal to the past. While working on the film, Jason gave that question a lot of thought. "You know, if I had a time machine, I don't know that I would go back and change anything as much as I would go back and relive past experiences," he told Scholastic News Online. "Honestly, if I could go back in time and redo *Minutemen*, like if I could re-film and live all those experiences again, I would, because it was so much fun."

The filming of *Minutemen* definitely represented a new high point in Jason's career. Disney was extremely impressed with his performance. In fact, in order to keep the Dolley/Disney relationship going, they were already offering him a voice-over part in the hit animated series *The Replacements*, which tells the story of the Daring siblings. The episode "Campiest Episode Ever" aired in May 2008. In that episode, Todd Daring goes to a camp where his sister Riley works as a camp counselor. Jason provided the voice for a camp counselor named Skip Tripper, who encourages Riley to be less responsible and just have fun. That episode was especially fun for Jason to shoot because he got to work with voice-over legend Nancy Cartwright, who also voices Bart Simpson on *The Simpsons*.

Jason met some incredible Disney talents working on *Minutemen*. Even after the shooting ended, the project just kept getting cooler. For example, when it came time to create the sound track, the producers turned to Disney veteran Corbin Bleu. The adorable star, who played Zac Efron's best bud Chad in *High School Musical*, recorded the film's opening track, an infectious tune called "Run It Back Again."

Minutemen finally had its premiere on the Disney Channel on January 25, 2008. For Jason, it was the culmination of a dream to reach Disney's inner circle. His future had always been bright. But now that he was the star of his own Disney film, it was positively blinding. And the rave reviews that *Minutemen* received from fans and critics only added to Jason's excitement. The *Montreal Gazette* called Jason and his costars "talents to watch for." Writing about Jason, the *Detroit Free Press* predicted that "*Minutemen* will be one of the first of many leading roles for this rising star." Jason was used to good press, but these accolades were out of sight!

After years of hard work, Jason was finally getting the kind of recognition he so deserved. But the tiny taste of fame was nothing compared with the mega-stardom he was about to attain.

CHAPTER 6

FANTASTIC FAME

Disney has made many young actors into international superstars. Thanks to the success of *Minutemen*, along with his ongoing role on *Cory in the House*, Jason was starting to become as famous as any Disney celebrity, past or present. In fact, even on the set of *Complete Savages*, he remembers running from a gang of fans, most of them female! "There's nothing quite like that," he admitted to Teenmag.com.

Maybe because of Mel Gibson's involvement,

Complete Savages really was the first time Jason appreciated how much attention celebrities receive. "When I first started on *Complete Savages*, I think people's interest in me was sparked a little bit—mainly the girls," he told Kidzworld.com. But now that Jason was a bona fide Disney celebrity, he was getting recognized everywhere he went. According to Teenmag.com, a fan even came up to him at Magic Mountain and said "Hi, picture?" Jason didn't realize what was going on, but before he knew it the fan had snapped a picture with his cell phone camera and disappeared.

By the time he was a teenager, Jason definitely had one of the most recognizable faces in show business. Or, should we say, one of the most recognizable heads of hair? "People came up to me to touch my hair!" he told DisneySociety.com when asked about some of his strangest early experiences with stardom. "People were like, 'Can I just touch it?' I'd be like, 'Why not?'"

That story pretty much sums up Jason's entire attitude toward stardom. Basically, he doesn't take

Hollywood seriously, so he's never going to get caught up in all the glitz and glamour. Even when he's around older, more established stars, like those he worked with on the set of *The Air I Breathe*, Jason keeps his cool. "I don't get starstruck," he told the *Detroit News*. "They are actors just like me. I see it as being in the same business."

Of course, Jason enjoys the perks of being a celebrity, including the handsome paychecks. But even with the steady cash he now has coming in, his only splurge to date was a home theater system he bought for his family back in California.

Jason also enjoys hanging out with other stars from Disney. "We don't hang out off-set a lot, but it's like Disney Channel high school," he told TeenHollywood.com. "You see people at events or you guest-star on shows together or do movies together and you get to know everybody. Everybody's really nice." Although, once he becomes close friends with a fellow star, Jason does see them as much as possible. "Maiara Walsh from *Cory in the House* lives in the same city I do and our families have gone out for sushi together. Jake Thomas also has spent the night at my house a couple of times." And how do the adorable costars spend the evening? "We go online and play video games together."

Video games are definitely a favorite activity among celebrities. Some actors are even lucky enough to have a console in their dressing rooms! On the set of *Cory in the House*, *Guitar Hero* seems to be the video game of choice. "Maiara has it set up in her dressing room," Jason told TeenHollywood.com. "I'm actually pretty good at it. I usually beat anybody that plays me."

As much as Jason likes hanging out with other celebrities, he hasn't turned his back on his old friends from California. That goes a long way toward keeping him grounded. "It is important to have friends outside of the business because they help you remember your roots," he told the *Detroit News*. Even though Jason's "regular" friends are aware of his celebrity, it hasn't changed the group dynamic. As he explained to

Newsday: "My friends will tell me, 'Oh, I bought a magazine and you were in it.' At the beginning it was kind of weird, but I'm kind of used to it now."

Jason also has plenty of interests outside of Hollywood. For starters, he's always been superclose with his family. He still hangs out a lot with his brothers, and his mom still accompanies him on photo shoots and press interviews. Then there are his many hobbies, including his newfound love of the guitar. Could music threaten to overtake his acting ambitions? "I think music is more of a hobby for me right now," Jason confided to DisneySociety.com. "I think acting will be the focus for me for the rest of my life—that's my dream. Things could change, but at this point no [music career]."

Another major distraction in Jason's life is the work he does helping others. Not only is he a caring, down-to-earth guy to his close friends, he's generous with strangers as well. On any given Saturday, he might be found at the Los Angeles Children's Hospital, hanging out with patients and signing autographs for their families.

Jason is also always ready with advice for actors younger than himself who are looking to break into show business. It might be something he picked up at Disney, where actors who have successfully risen through the ranks look out for the next generation of up-and-comers. Jason's advice is always pretty straightforward: "Take classes," he once told the readers of Kidzworld.com. "[Acting] is not as easy as it looks . . . It's far from glamorous but if you really love it then it's a lot of fun. But it really is a lot of work—especially with school. I find I have to work a lot harder than I would if I wasn't an actor to keep up with school."

Jason is one of the hottest young stars in Hollywood, with roles pouring in, legions of fans, and a trophy case full of awards to prove it. But to listen to him talk, he sounds more like the cool upperclassmen—the smart, handsome guy who is bound for the top college. In fact, that's not so far from the truth! "I do plan to go to college and get a degree, so if acting doesn't work out, I'll have something solid to fall back on," he told Kidzworld.com.

It's hard to imagine other stars in Hollywood talking like that. They're more concerned about fancy clothes and the party scene. But for Jason Dolley, acting is not about being famous. It's about doing what he loves. And it's because of his down-to-earth devotion to his craft that Jason Dolley is shaping up to be one of the best actors of his generation.

CHAPTER 7

GIRLS, GIRLS, GIRLS

Jason Dolley is famous for his on-screen chemistry with female costars, whether he's cracking jokes with Maiara Walsh on *Cory in the House* or sharing a heartfelt moment with Kay Panabaker in the movie *Read It And Weep*. But that's all just acting. What's Jason like in real life when it comes to relationships? The answer, much to the delight of young ladies everywhere, is that he's always been a total romantic!

Actually, Jason's parents didn't let him officially start dating seriously until he was sixteen, but that didn't stop him from having crushes, or from enjoying his first kiss two years earlier. "I was 14," he told *Seventeen*. "It was on the set of *Read It and Weep*." That's right—his first kiss was for work! The scene comes at the end of the movie, after Kay Panabaker's character asks Jason's character for forgiveness. They seal their reconciliation with a tender smooch on the school dance floor. "The practice kiss was my first one," Jason recalled. "It was really cool."

But that's still just acting. What about *real*-life romance? Although rumors are constantly swirling around the Hollywood heartthrob, Jason hasn't been spotted with any steady girlfriends. He has, however, made it perfectly clear what he's looking for in love. "There's a rule that I have to keep," he told *Tiger Beat*. "The girl I want is someone who will love me for who I am—no matter what." What's not to love? But Jason's requirements don't stop there. "I'd also want someone who's not afraid to try new things," he continued. "I love sushi, so she has to be willing to try it. I love to travel, so she has to like doing that and have the freedom to do it." Got that, ladies?

In terms of physical looks, Jason seems to go for long hair and an athletic body type. For example, when *Seventeen* asked who his celebrity crush is, he settled right away on Jessica Alba. "Even though I just read she has a fiancé, it doesn't matter," he said. "It's not like something I would actually pursue. I mean, I would *try* asking her out, but that would never work. She's *really* pretty; she's a really good actress, too."

Despite joking about going after Jessica Alba (who's already taken!), Jason has pretty traditional attitudes when it comes to relationships. For example, he once bought a girl sixteen roses for her sixteenth birthday. And he's often the one who does the asking out, following the old-fashioned tradition. But that doesn't mean he's against a more modern approach. "It's not a problem when a girl asks me out," he told *BOP* magazine. "All it means is that I don't have to go up to her and ask her. It's definitely not traditional, but it happens. Times have changed."

Jason is definitely an enlightened, twenty-first

century guy. He even enjoys hitting the stores. "Guys like to shop," he told *BOP* magazine. "Guys don't like to shop for the same things girls do, like clothes and perfume. Guys shop at places like Best Buy." Still, just getting a guy to a mall used to be impossible. But not Jason!

Although Jason does like hanging out at the mall, it's not his ideal setting for a date. Unless, that is, it's a mall with lots of awesome restaurants. "I like to eat!" he exclaimed on TV.com. "Food is awesome. So we'd go for a meal." But for a first date, he might go somewhere with a little more action, like an amusement park. "If you're still sort of getting to know her, there's more stuff going on at amusement parks than at dinner. And I love roller coasters."

Jason's other advice for first-time dating is to make it a group activity. He thinks its a great idea to take some friends along on a first date so its more relaxed and everyone can have fun. "Group dating allows you to get to know somebody," he said to DisneySociety.com. "Even if it's just one girl in the group that you like.

I think you get to know her and hang out with her and have fun without having to worry about the commitment. Group dates take the pressure off the situation."

For a guy who hasn't been in many serious relationships, Jason sure knows a lot about love. That may have something to do with his July 5 birthday, which makes him a Cancer star sign. Cancers are known to be emotional, loving, and romantic, qualities that Jason has also displayed. Cancers are also extremely sensitive and intuitive, which promises to make Jason as good a boyfriend as he is an actor.

One thing is certain: Jason knows how to treat a girl right. "I don't ignore girls," he told *BOP* magazine, although he understands why some guys might do it. "If a guy is ignoring you, it could be he likes you," Jason said. "Guys will be embarrassed that they like a girl. If they tease you a lot, they probably like you."

Jason sure gets relationships, even if for the moment he feels he's too young and too busy with his career to pursue love seriously. But when he does finally meet the right girl, he'll be ready with all the right moves. As he's learned, being famous may get you a lot of adoring fans, but it can't guarantee love. Even celebrities "still gotta work [their] stuff," Jason told Kidzworld.com. "Some things never change." Luckily, Jason is willing to work hard to win his dream girl's heart when the time comes!

CHAPTER 8

A REGULAR KID

Jason's skills in front of the camera, not to mention his charming ways with the ladies, definitely make him a superstar. Throw in the 4.0 grade point average Jason maintains at school, and he almost starts to seem superhuman. It's true that Jason is definitely one of the biggest talents of his generation, but deep down inside, he's actually a pretty regular American kid.

Don't believe it? Consider that his breakfast of choice isn't something fancy, like fresh-squeezed orange juice and flaky croissants flown in from France, but rather a big bowl of Wheaties! It doesn't get much more all-American than that.

Following breakfast, Jason might turn on his iPod while he gets dressed for the day. His interests in music are pretty diverse, from the Beatles to Ozzy Osbourne to the Counting Crows. Most days, he slips into a pair of broken-in Levis 529 jeans (he loves them so much that he actually has four pairs!). On top, he might put on a graphic tee from his favorite store, Fossil, over a well-worn long-sleeve shirt. Jason's style is cool but casual, the perfect duds for his active lifestyle.

When he's not shooting a film or television show, Jason's hobbies include sports like football and soccer. But he's also into a lot of alternative activities, including hacky sack and yo-yo. "It's hard because the traditional sports are the ones that schools offer, so if you want to try something else you really have to go looking for it," he told *PBS Kids*. "With hacky sack, somebody brought one to recess in sixth grade and it kind of all went downhill from there! The same with the yo-yos! One kid brought a yo-yo one day and people started getting them. I just kept at it and found that I really loved it."

As with acting, when Jason puts his mind to something, he usually becomes one of the best at it. His costars on *Cory in the House* will attest to the fact that he's nearly impossible to beat at the video game *Guitar Hero*. And he's pretty much a virtuoso with the yo-yo—but only after years of practice. "I think my favorite trick to do is called a barrel roll," he said to Scholastic News Online. "When I was first learning yo-yo tricks—you know, the Walk the Dog and Rock the Baby and Eiffel Tower and all that—I never heard of a barrel roll and I had no idea what it was . . . And people see you take out your yo-yo and they expect stuff like Walk the Dog or Rock the Baby, like they expect you to be able to Rock the Baby for like a minute, but then you do [the barrel roll] and then they go—their whole idea of yo-yoing is turned upside down. That's awesome. I love that!"

Jason's quirky talents don't stop with the yo-yo. He's also a master of the Rubik's Cube, the colorful mechanical puzzle that was invented in 1974 by a Hungarian sculptor and architecture professor named Ernó Rubik. Most people find the puzzle impossible to solve, but not Jason. In fact, he can solve his Rubik's Cube in under a minute! "Fastest record, I think, was 37 seconds," he reported to Scholastic News Online. "Usually about a minute. I haven't been practicing as much lately. Probably I could still get it in about a minute, but my record was 37 seconds." So what's Jason's secret? Does it have to do with the fact that he's a whiz at math in school? "There's a formula," he admits. "But it's got to do with patterns. A lot of people will think that there's math involved. I don't really think there's math as much as there is memorizing steps. Because at the end, it gets to the point where you just have to see where you have to put everything and then you have to do a set of moves, that's literally how I solve it . . . It's complicated."

The Rubik's Cube may be complicated for some, but not for Jason. However, don't think it's something Jason mastered without even trying. "It took me two years to master my hidden talent," Jason confessed to *Tiger Beat.* For Jason, the Rubik's Cube is a lot like acting. He makes it looks easy, but the truth is he had to work incredibly hard to get to that level.

Jason's regular-kid personality is revealed in other ways. Although his dream car is a Chevy Camaro Concept, he drives a more practical Honda Civic (although he did request custom rims!).

Jason may have the cool-guy looks of a rebel, but the truth is he lives life responsibly. He goes to church regularly, and until his busy acting schedule forced him into homeschooling, he had attended a Christian school in his town of Simi Valley. Jason attributes his down-to-earth attitude to the influence of the church. "Most of the people there I've known all my life and I can go there and just be one of the guys," he said to *PBS Kids.* "These people know me as me. It means so much to have that in my life." Jason is so devoted to religion that when TeenHollywood.com asked what era in time he would like to travel back to, he answered, "I would love to be at the Sermon on the Mount or any of Christ's speeches or just follow him around and hang out with him a bit." Jason may never fulfill that desire, but it's enough for him to be active in youth group, where he enjoys helping out younger kids with their Bible studies.

Jason does have some bad habits, but they're not what you often hear from famous actors. He doesn't smoke or drink, and he certainly doesn't do drugs. So what is Jason's number one vice? "For the most part I've kicked it, but I would pull on my nails," he confessed to *Seventeen*. "If they got to a certain length, I would pull them off before cutting them. But I'm pretty sure it's done."

Jason's other guilty pleasure is sweets. He has a serious weakness for chocolate chip cookie dough ice cream, and he's also a huge fan of Reese's Peanut Butter Cups. After a long day of acting, his favorite thing is to plop down on the sofa and watch "a show on The History Channel called 'Monster Quest,'" he told *Seventeen*. "It's where they go and look for the Big Foot and stuff like that. Some of the episodes are really out there, but it's entertaining. I like to watch it." Jason also enjoys surfing the Internet, especially the site homestarrunner.com. "Basically, it's cartoon characters and they've got different episodes and it's really funny," he said. "Check it out!"

When shooting ends for the season, Jason loves nothing more than going on long vacations with his family. Disneyland in California is a favorite destination if the Dolleys only have a few days to work with. But for longer holidays, Jason opts for a cruise every time. Jason loves the ocean, so spending a week or more on the open sea is sheer delight. "I went on a cruise in the Caribbean, and that was some of the most amazing snorkeling I have ever done," Jason told Scholastic News Online. "There are some incredible fish in the Caribbean. I'd just love to follow one . . . I won't try to touch it or anything. I'll just watch it like I used to do when I was fishing. I just stare at the fish. I can watch them for hours . . . I could spend an entire day out there snorkeling. The water is so blue when you're looking at it from the top, and it's so clear when you're in it. It's unbelievable."

Jason's love of the sea is so intense that if he ever stops working as an actor, he would consider a career somehow related to the ocean. "I think something like a marine biologist would be really cool," he told Scholastic News Online. "Because that kind of science has always been particularly fascinating and interesting . . . I've always loved going to aquariums. So, something in that field, I don't even know what I would do, but something dealing with fish or marine life or something like that would be incredible."

A career in politics also appeals to Jason. "Not necessarily the president, though," he admitted to Scholastic News Online. "Politicians have grueling interviews and I'd like to see what that's like because it would be very interesting! They have to be completely behind everything they say . . . You know, I would go for fixing world hunger or world peace . . . "

And if politics and marine biology didn't work out? "I always thought I would be a teacher," he said to *Seventeen*. "I think it would be cool to be the person who's assigning homework! But if I can act for the rest of my life, that's what I want to do."

For the time being, Jason's acting career is pretty solid. In fact, when he's in the middle of a busy shoot, his day doesn't end until 10 P.M.! The life of a professional actor is so demanding that Jason has a hard time understanding how some celebrities can get into trouble with drugs and alcohol. "I work all day, so when I get home I'm tired," he told *PBS Kids.* "I don't really go out and party."

Jason may be too tired to hit the party scene—a fact his parents definitely appreciate—but Jason's busy schedule doesn't mean they let him get out of doing chores. "I pick up after my chocolate Labrador Jasmine," he told TV.com. "I make my bed. I don't take out the trash a lot, but I used to shred papers for my mom, who is an accountant." As for cooking, Jason leaves the complicated dishes to Mom and Dad (or the chef at his favorite restaurant!). But when Jason has a late-night snack attack, he can definitely take care of himself. "I can make a really good tuna melt and a really nice garlic grilled cheese sandwich!" he explained to TV.com. Yum!

All in all, Jason's life isn't that much different than that of the average American teen. Sure, he's one of the biggest stars of his generation. But if you were to run into Jason on the street, he'd probably seem like any kid from school. And he'd expect you to treat him that way. "Hey if you ever see me, don't be afraid to say hi," he told *BOP*. Spoken like a true regular guy!

CHAPTER 9

THE FUTURE TENSE

By the time Jason turned seventeen, he had already accomplished more than some actors accomplish in a lifetime, but he shows no sign of slowing down. In fact, when it comes to his career, Jason is just getting warmed up! *Forbes* magazine actually named Jason as one of Eight Hot Young Kid Stars To Watch, along with the biggest kids in the business like the Jonas Brothers, Selena Gomez, and Chelsea Staub. That's one awesome list!

Jason appreciated the shout-out from *Forbes*, but

even without its seal of approval, there's plenty he wants to accomplish for his own satisfaction. For starters, there are still many Hollywood bigwigs he wants to work with. Who tops the list? "I have two answers for that—actor and director," he told Kidzworld.com. "My favorite actor is Liam Neeson. His performance in *Batman Begins* just blew me away. Also, the director I'd really love to work with is M. Night Shyamalan—*Signs*, *Sixth Sense*, all of those—they're such great mind thrillers. I love his style and I'd love to be part of one of his movies."

Working with Neeson and Shyamalan, as well as his other favorite actor/director, Robert Redford, is part of Jason's long-term plan. But he'll have plenty to keep him busy in the short-term as well, including the release of his next Disney original movie called *Hatching Pete*, scheduled to come out in spring of 2009.

Hatching Pete is another Disney production. Jason plays the part of Pete, a painfully shy student who ends up being the school mascot when his best friend, Cleatis (played by Mitchel Musso), has to give up the job because he's allergic to the costume. Pete and Cleatis initially decide to keep the switch a secret. But then Cleatis becomes one of the most popular kids in school. "I do a great job and kind of come out of my shell, while Mitchel gets all the credit," Jason explained to *PBS Kids*. "So we kind of switch places and obviously it affects our friendship. It's a really cool story!" In the end, Pete has to make a tough decision: Does he reveal his true identity and risk his friendship with Cleatis? Or keep up the secret and remain the kid that nobody pays any attention to? The movie should really keep audiences on the edge of their seats.

Hatching Pete was filmed on location at Hillcrest High School in Utah. That's not far from where *Minutemen* was filmed, so it all must have felt pretty familiar to Jason. But he got to work with a brand-new cast of actors, including Mitchel Musso, who audiences will recognize from his work in *Hannah Montana*, where he plays the part of Oliver Oscar Oken.

The costars have a lot in common, so they must have enjoyed working together. For starters, Mitchel was born on July 9, 1991, just four days after Jason!

Both actors have a pet dog (Jason has his chocolate Lab Jasmine and Mitchel has a pooch named Stitch). And they're both super into music. In fact, Musso has done professional recordings, and he's even been on tour with Raven-Symoné. Jason must have enjoyed jamming with his costar during downtimes on the set of *Hatching Pete*!

Jason has high hopes for *Hatching Pete*. If it does as well as *Minutemen*, his reputation as one of Disney's biggest stars will pretty much be guaranteed. More Disney roles will be sure to follow, although Jason's ambitions go beyond the Disney Channel. He once told *Newsday* that he "wants a guest spot on *The Simpsons*," the hit animated series on Fox that features the lovable Bart Simpson.

Jason would also like to work on some period pieces, especially something set in the Wild West. "I've always loved westerns," he told *Popstar!* "I'd love to play the cowboy and save the day." That hasn't changed since Jason was little! The world of fantasy also appeals to Jason. "Oooo, I wish I could have been a part of *The*

Lord of the Rings," he said to TeenHollywood.com. "That would be amazing."

Obviously, there are still plenty of roles Jason wants to play before he'll be ready to give up acting. Considering how cute and talented he is, his fans are hoping he never runs out of parts!

CHAPTER 10

JASON GOES GREEN

Jason is committed to acting. But there's one thing he takes more seriously: saving the planet. Jason is a huge supporter of the green movement, which refers to people who are devoted to being environmentally conscious. Jason has been on board with the movement ever since he noticed how polluted the air in his home state of California had become. "If I'm driving to work sometimes, I can just look over the San Fernando Valley and there's always smog," he told Scholastic News Online. That was an upsetting

revelation for the young star.

For a nature-lover like Jason, the pollution was unacceptable. Fortunately, lots of people in Hollywood feel the same way, so Jason isn't alone in his efforts to save the planet. In April 2008, just in time for Earth Day, Jason got together with several other Disney stars to raise awareness about the environment. On-hand with Jason was Mitchel Musso, his costar from *Hatching Pete*; Maiara Walsh from *Cory in the House*; Selena Gomez and David Henrie, stars of the show *Wizards of Waverly Place*; and Alyson Stoner of *Camp Rock* fame.

Jason and his fellow environmentalists are always looking for ways to keep the planet green. "I think that's what I would say for kids to do is just kind of look around and do a little research about what's actually going on in your area or in any area," he told Scholastic News Online. "Do some research and I'm sure the websites or books or whatever will give you some ideas." Here are nine tips to get you started going green:

☐ **UNPLUG ELECTRONICS.** Even when electronic devices are turned off, some of them still use electricity. "Turn off all of your TVs and gadgets and gizmos in your house," Jason said to the *East Valley Tribune*. "They all have a stand-by mode, but that uses up a lot of power."

☐ **CARRY AROUND REUSABLE CANVAS BAGS WHEN YOU GO SHOPPING.** This will keep plastic and paper bags out of the landfills. "We've seen that we can start by making simple changes like packing our lunch with reusable bags and utensils," Selena Gomez said to the *East Valley Tribune*.

☐ **CHANGE A LIGHTBULB.** A compact fluorescent bulb uses 70 percent less energy than a standard incandescent bulb. Maiara Walsh explained to the *East Valley Tribune*, "Using energy-saving bulbs is easy and efficient." Besides conserving energy, compact fluorescent bulbs end up saving money in the long run, a fact your parents will definitely appreciate!

☐ **RECYCLE.** Instead of throwing plastic and glass containers into the garbage, set them aside for curbside collection. "My number one thing is to recycle everything from newspaper to aluminum cans," said Alyson Stoner in the *East Valley Tribune.*

☐ **START A COMPOST BIN.** That way, you can throw food scraps onto the compost pile, instead of tossing them into the trash. When Mitchel Musso gardens with his grandma, "the leftover green cuttings go in the compost bin," he told the *East Valley Tribune*.

☐ **REDUCE PAPER WASTE.** "Use every inch of both

sides of the paper while taking class notes," said Selena Gomez in the *East Valley Tribune*. Sending an e-mail instead of a letter is another way to reduce how much paper you create. When you do have to use paper, be sure to recycle it once you're done with it.

☐ **PLANT A TREE.** Trees help clean the air and they also prevent soil erosion. If you plant a tree with lots of leaves in front of a window, it will also keep your house cool during the summer. Why not organize a tree-planting party with a bunch of your friends? Arbor Day, which is the last Friday in April, is the perfect date.

☐ **PUT YOUR COMPUTER TO SLEEP.** Using the sleep mode on your PC will cause it to automatically conserve power when it's not in use. According to the Environmental

Protection Agency, putting your computer to sleep can save seventy dollars worth of electricity!

- [ ] **DON'T PRERINSE DISHES.** If loading the dishwasher after dinner is one of your regular chores, don't rinse them in the sink first. It's a waste of water, since the dishwasher will clean the dishes just fine without you rinsing them first.

CHAPTER 11

Could You and Jason Be BFFs?

How great would it be to count Jason Dolley among your closest friends? He's loyal, fun, kind, compassionate—pretty much everything you look for in a BFF. Friends are an important part of Jason's life, whether it's the gang from school in Simi Valley that he's hung out with for years, or the new costars he meets on the sets of Disney and Hollywood studios like Maiara Walsh and Mitchel Musso.

But what about *you*? Are you the kind of person Jason would find compatible? He's definitely up for

meeting new people and making new friends. But that doesn't mean he'll pal around with just anyone. There are certain qualities he looks for in his friends. By taking the following personality quiz, you can find out what you do (or don't) have in common with the fabulous Jason Dolley. Good luck!

1. YOUR IDEA OF A PERFECT WEEKEND AFTERNOON IS:

A. heading to the amusement park with friends and hitting all the wildest, stomach-turning rides until your pals are begging for mercy.

B. getting ahead on that massive book report for school and redecorating your room *before* taking off to check out the latest exhibit at the local museum.

C. Planting trees for the environment with a group of cool kids.

2. IF YOU WERE A CAR, HERE'S WHAT TYPE YOU WOULD BE:

A. a hot, red convertible sports car that was made to go 100 mph.

B. an SUV that works equally well off-road in the bumpy, country hillside or rolling up to a cool city restaurant.

C. a hybrid that's not only energy-efficient but also very fashionable.

3. ANYONE WHO'S YOUR BFF NEEDS TO:

A. be able to stay up all night playing games, cracking jokes, and telling stories at a sleepover.

B. take schoolwork seriously and enjoy a wide range of fun extracurricular activities.

C. be up on current events and feel passionately about some social issues.

4. IF YOU WON A MILLION DOLLARS, YOU WOULD:

A. plan a weeklong adventure trip for you, your family, and all your friends.

B. set aside money for college, and take an investment class to learn the best way to manage and grow the rest of your cash.

C. make huge donations to all your favorite charities, and boy are there a lot of them!

5. YOUR ROLE MODELS TEND TO BE:

A. glamorous superstars who fly their own planes and world-class athletes who like to play really hard.

B. inventors with brilliant ideas and successful CEOs of major companies
C. kids who take a year off before going to college in order to do community service and make the world a better place.

6. THE FIRST THING YOU DO AT A BIRTHDAY PARTY IS:

A. grab a bunch of the guests and get one of the games going.
B. introduce yourself to the parents hosting the party.
C. go over and talk to the kid who doesn't know anyone at the party.

7. YOUR FRIENDS RELY ON YOU TO:

A. wear zany outfits to school, whether they match or not.
B. help with the superhard math homework set that no one else can figure out.
C. speak and stand up to a bully during recess when everyone is freaking out.

8. YOUR FANTASY PET IS:

A. a snow leopard.

B. a thoroughbred horse

C. a panda bear.

9. ONE THING YOUR PARENTS WILL NEVER CATCH YOU DOING IS:

A. sleeping until noon on a beautiful Saturday afternoon.

B. leaving the extra-credit portion on any test blank.

C. spending all your allowance on yourself.

10. YOU FEEL YOUR BEST WHEN:

A. you're moving as fast as you can.

B. you're thinking as hard as you can.

C. you're helping someone out the most that you can.

IF YOU ANSWERED MOSTLY AS:

You and Jason share an adventurous streak. If you and he were friends, there definitely wouldn't be very many dull moments in your relationship. Camping trips, deep-sea diving, paintball outings—you'd do it all. In fact, the rest

of the friends in your group would probably have trouble keeping up with you and Jason!

IF YOU ANSWERED MOSTLY BS:

Your ambitious side would definitely appeal to Jason. You and he would spend most of your time engaged in activities aimed at bettering yourselves—study groups, field trips to monuments and museums, and hours in front of the TV watching the History Channel. You and Jason would have plenty of fun, of course, but there'd be meaning and purpose behind every activity as well. But then you'd go celebrate with burgers and fries!

IF YOU ANSWERED MOSTLY CS:

Your friendship with Jason would be all about making the world a better place. At school, you'd be most likely to organize an Earth Day event, or a fundraiser to help improve the library, or a campaign to increase your community's recycling efforts. Anytime Jason attended events aimed at raising awareness about social issues, he'd invite you to come along. Pretty cool, huh?

CHAPTER 12

FUN FACTS

Think you're Jason's biggest fan? You're not the only one. After all, millions of kids tune in each week to watch him on *Cory in the House*. And millions more watched *Read it and Weep*, *Minutemen*, and the other movies he's made. That means a lot of competition for number one fan honors. To even have a chance, you definitely need to know these fun facts. That way, you'll not only be in the running to be Jason's biggest fan, you'll also know what to order if someday you end up ahead of him in line at the snack bar and want to buy him his favorite candy bar. Jason always says he likes his fans to come up and say hello to him. But if you're holding his favorite sweet, he'll be *really* happy to see you!

BIOGRAPHICAL TRIVIA

Full name: Jason Scott Dolley

Height: 6' 0"

Eye color: Blue

Birth date: July 5, 1991

Hometown: Simi Valley, California

Best subjects in school: Bible studies and science

First commercial: Smorz cereal

Closest sibling: His brother Jeffrey

FAVORITE ACTIVITIES

Outdoor game: Airsoft

Instrument: The guitar

Sports: Football, baseball, basketball

Hobbies: Paintball, yo-yo, Rubik's cube

Board game: *Settlers of Catan*

FAVORITE FELLOW CELEBRITIES

Actor: Liam Neeson

Comedian: Lou Costello

Personal idol: Robert Redford

Director: M. Night Shyamalan

FAVORITE ENTERTAINMENT

TV show: *The Simpsons*

Movie: *The Lord of the Rings* trilogy

Book: *The Lion, the Witch, and the Wardrobe,* by C.S. Lewis

Video game: *Guitar Hero*

Website: Homestarrunner.com

Rock band: Counting Crows

Song: "Last Words" by Thousand Foot Crutch

FAVORITE FOODS

Ice cream: Chocolate chip cookie dough

Pizza: Sausage

Foreign food: Sushi

American food: Double-Double from In-N-Out Burger

Cereal: Wheaties

Candy bar: Reese's Peanut Butter Cups

ODDS AND ENDS

Favorite feature on a girl: Her smile

Favorite city: New York City

Favorite store: Fossil

Worst habit: Pulling his nails

CHAPTER 13

INTERNET RESOURCES

You know as much about Jason Dolley as anyone on the planet (well, except for maybe his mom and dad!). But Jason is constantly taking on new projects and discovering new passions. While *Cory in the House* will hopefully stay on the air for years, Jason could end up starring in a whole new series. Or he might finally get tired of the Rubik's Cube and pick up a new hobby. Or his guitar playing might reach a level where he's ready to start going on tour, maybe even with Mitchel Musso or one of his musical costars. We're not saying those things will happen. But they might! So you need to stay on top of the latest information about Jason. Here's a list of websites that are chock-full of the latest facts about Jason. Make sure you always get a parent's permission before you go online. Bookmark these sites today and you'll always be the first to know when something new and exciting happens in the life of Jason Dolley!

http://profile.myspace.com/index.cfm?fuseaction=user.viewprofile&friendid=148086097

Jason's MySpace page

http://www.jasondolley.com

Jason's official fan site

http://www.jason-dolley.net/

Another fan site devoted to all things Jason Dolley

http://tv.disney.go.com/disneychannel/originalmovies/minutemen/

The official *Minutemen* page

http://tv.disney.go.com/disneychannel/coryin the house/

The official *Cory in the House* page

http://en.wikipedia.org/wiki/Jason_Dolley

Jason's Wikipedia page

http://www.imdb.com/name/nm1591666/

Jason's page on the Internet Movie Database

http://theairibreathemovie.com/

The official website for the film *The Air I Breathe*

CHECK OUT THESE OTHER HOT STARS!